# Missy

## The Cat Who Loves To Eat Vegetables

JOHNNY WANG

# DEDICATION

This book is dedicated to my daughter. I hope she will always be happy just like all the other kids in the world!

# ACKNOWLEDGMENTS

Thanks to my wife and family for taking care of our kids so I have the time to make this book published and share to all the kids in the world.

Missy was a cat who lives in the city

She didn't like to eat vegetables and would push away her plate with veggies.

One day, Missy received a letter from her cousin, Mimi.

Mimi was inviting Missy to visit her in the farm.

Missy was so excited that she started to pack her things.

Missy was so anxious to meet Mimi again because it's been a while since the last time she saw her cousin.

Finally, after a long trip, Missy and Mimi met.

Both of them were so happy to see each other.

On her stay, Mimi toured Missy around the farm

where Missy saw a lot of different vegetables in varying colors and shapes.

Missy saw Mimi eating some of the vegetables.

Missy asked Mimi why she liked to eat them. Mimi had several reasons why she likes to eat veggies.

# #1

Eating veggies helps YOU grow taller.

# Mimi was taller than Missy

so Mimi could reach higher.

# #2

## Vegetables provide YOU with more energy.

# With more energy…

Mimi could run faster.

# #3

## Veggies help YOU flight diseases.

Veggies helped Mimi recover from her sickness.

so Mimi could play outside much often.

# #4

Veggies improve how YOUR skin looks and overall body appearance.

Because of the nutrition in the veggies,

Mimi looked more beautiful with healthy eyes, skin and hair.

# #5

## Veggies help you become stronger.

# With more strength and power…

Mimi could hang on bars longer.

# #6

## Vegetables make YOU smarter.

# By eating veggies…

Mimi could do her homework faster.

Mimi encouraged Missy to try eating some veggies.

Missy wasn't willing but Mimi reminded Missy all the good things eating veggies do.

# Missy tried and surprisingly…

Missy found herself enjoying carrots, peas and broccolis.

# Time passed by quickly…

… it's now time for Missy to go home and say her goodbyes to Mimi.

Missy now loves to eat vegetables just like her cousin Mimi.

She tries to cook vegetables by herself.

After weeks of eating healthy veggies…

Missy is now a beautiful, healthy and energetic cat.

# ABOUT THE AUTHOR

Johnny Wang who lives in Taiwan is a father of two lovely kids, a daughter and a son. He works in a regular 9-5 day job and during his free time, he'd like to come up with some ideas publishing his own books. The idea of this book came from her daughter, Sunny who especially loves the color of blue, so that's why the main cat is blue!!

CPSIA information can be obtained
at www.ICGtesting.com
Printed in the USA
BVHW020803180720
584023BV00011B/453

* 9 7 8 1 5 1 5 2 7 7 6 6 8 *